SWASHBY and the SEA

written by **BETH FERRY**

illustrated by **JUANA MARTINEZ-NEAL**

HOUGHTON MIFFLIN HARCOURT

Boston New York

For Art and Marsha—neighbors . . . friends . . . family —B. F.

To Aidan, my favorite sea captain —J. M-N.

hmhbooks.com

The illustrations for this book were done in acrylics, colored pencils, and graphite on hand-textured paper.
The text type was set in Chapparal Pro.
The display type was set in Catalina Avalon Slab.

Library of Congress Control Number: 2018052169

ISBN: 978-0-544-70737-5

Manufactured in China
SCP 10 9 8 7 6
4500831475

CAPTAIN SWASHBY loved the sea.

The sea and he had been friends for a long, long time.

She knew him in and out,

    up and down,

        and better than anyone.

So when Swashby retired, it was to a small house
on a small beach as close to the sea as he could be.
    Whenever he needed something, the sea provided
exactly the right thing at exactly the right time.
    Life was just the way Swashby liked it.
    Salty
        and sandy
            and serene.
                Until . . .

squeaks and squeals sprang from the empty house
next door.
Which was no longer empty.

It had been commandeered by a girl and her granny,
who planted umbrellas,
    scattered beach chairs,
        AND boarded Swashby's deck without permission!

Swashby battened down the hatches,
hid when the doorbell rang, and fed their
oatmeal cookies to the gulls.
   He didn't need neighbors.
   He didn't want neighbors.
   Neighbors were nosy,
      a nuisance,
            annoying.

So, in return, he left a message written clearly in the sand,

NO TRESPASSING

which the sea fiddled with, just a little bit.

"SING," the girl read.
And did just that.

She sang every song she knew while dancing up and down Swashby's deck.

"What now?" she asked.

"NOW VANISH!" Swashby wrote later that evening, adding a starfish exclamation point.

And the sea fiddled, just a little.

"W—ISH," the girl read, picking up the starfish.

And did just that.

She closed her eyes, and began, "I wish—"

"No, no," Swashby interrupted, stomping down the steps.

"If ye mean to make a starfish wish, ye must say this:

"Starfish back to waves so blue.

The sea will see a wish come true."

"How lovely," Granny said.
"We wish you'd come for a cup of tea,
Mr. Swashby."

But Swashby wished to be left alone,
so he grumbled and mumbled and
hurried inside.
He didn't need tea.
He didn't want tea.
Tea was civilized,
    friendly,
        neighborly.

What he needed was a new message.

PLEASE GO AWAY

he wrote firmly in the sand.

And, once again, the sea fiddled, just a little.

"PL—AY!" the girl sounded out, and did just that—with Swashby's shells and stones, with his buckets and shovels.

But her towers kept falling.

"Barnacle bottoms," Swashby muttered, marching out. "Yer doing it all wrong! Ye must not use the sun-baked sand. It's the sea sand does the trick."

And he showed her how to dig for the wet sand below.

"Thank—"
But Swashby was gone.

Before long, amazing sculptures decorated the beach.

"It's the clam shells ye should be usin'," Swashby called from inside.

"Come play, Mr. Swashby," the girl called back.

"Swashbys don't play," he answered, banging the shutters.

So the sea decided to meddle more than just a little.
She inched her way up the sand and tickled the girl's toes.
She nibbled on the sculptures and slurped away the bucket.

The girl tried to grab it, but . . .
"Look at me!" the girl called.
"Look at her!" Granny gasped.
"Oh dear, look at her."
Granny hurried to the water's edge, but . . .

Swashby was already there.

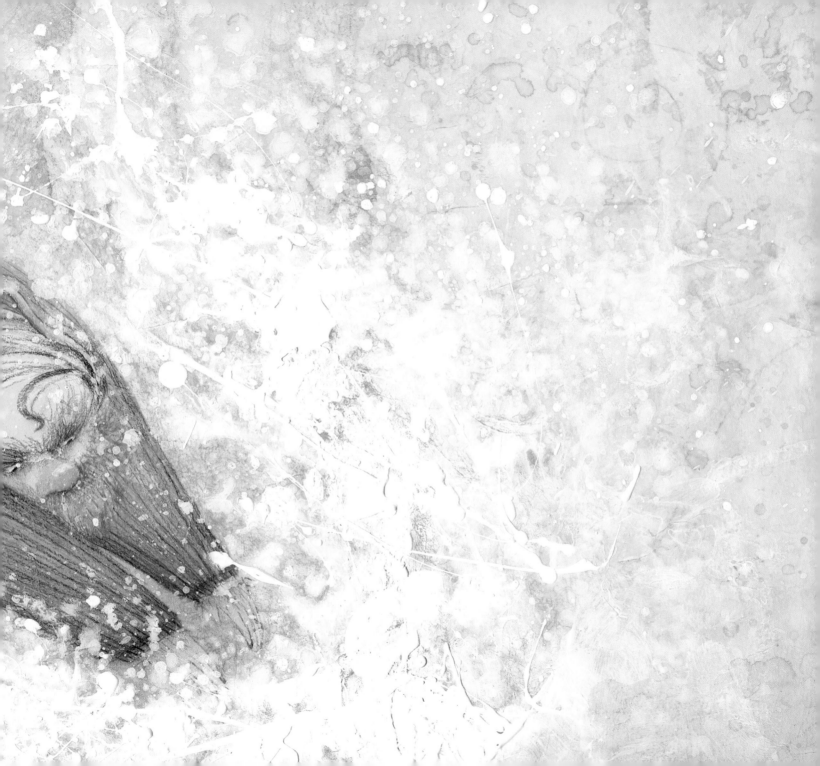

"What are ye up to, ye great salty imp?" he asked, scooping up the girl and the bucket.

With a great big wave, the sea delivered the pair back to shore.

And there was no stopping the laughing and thanking and hugging that was Swashby's reward.

"I see what ye did," he whispered to the sea as he was whisked away to celebrate.

After that, it was easy for Swashby to have tea with
the girl and her granny—
and ice cream,
and lobster,
and s'mores on the beach.
It was easy for him to share his special sea glass.
It was even easy for him to see that neighbors
could be fun,
and friends,
and . . . family.

And when he had a moment to himself, Swashby
carved a heartfelt message for the sea,

THANK YE, FRIEND

which the sea fiddled with, just a little bit.